Little Golden Books
Little Golden Books
Little Golden Books
Little Golden Books
Little Golden Books

a Little Golden Book® Collectio

Nine Disney Classics

A GOLDEN BOOK • NEW YORK

Published in the United States by Golden Books, an imprint of Random House Children's Books,
a division of Penguin Random House LLC, 1745 Broadway, New York, NY 10019,
and in Canada by Penguin Random House Canada Limited, Toronto,
in conjunction with Disney Enterprises, Inc.
The stories in this book were originally published separately in different form by Golden Books as
Mickey Mouse and His Spaceship in 1952, 2016; *Little Man of Disneyland* in 1955, 2015;
Mad Hatter's Tea Party in 1951, 2016; *The Sword in the Stone* in 1963, 2015;
Cinderella's Friends in 1950, 2017; *The Lucky Puppy* in 1960, 2017; *Mary Poppins* in 1964, 2016;
Sleeping Beauty and the Good Fairies in 1958, 2018; and *The Ugly Duckling* in 1952, 2017.

rhcbooks.com

ISBN 978-0-7364-3788-2

MANUFACTURED IN CHINA

10 9 8 7 6 5 4 3 2 1

Contents

WALT DISNEY'S

MICKEY MOUSE

AND HIS SPACE-SHIP

"Listen to this," said Mickey Mouse as he read from the evening paper. "'Big Contest! Fifty-Thousand-Dollar Prize for First Round Trip to Moon.'"

"Oh, Mickey!" cried Minnie Mouse. "Think how dangerous it would be!"

"Think how wonderful it would be!" cried Mickey. "I hope Donald Duck and I can get our spaceship finished in time!"

Mickey and Donald sped up the work on their spaceship. They were building it in an old factory at the edge of town.

"Be sure not to mention this to anyone, Donald," Mickey said in a serious tone. "There will be plenty of people trying to get that prize."

Donald promised. But he ran into Goofy the very next day.

"Coming to my birthday party next week?" asked Goofy.

"I don't know," said Donald smugly. "I might be on my way to the moon then."

Donald didn't notice the tough-looking fellow nearby. Pegleg Pete had heard everything. He slyly followed Donald to the factory and saw the spaceship Donald and Mickey were working on.

Mickey and Donald worked day and night, checking their instruments and launching gear, and finally laying in supplies.

At last everything was in order.

"Tomorrow is the big day," said Mickey. "We'll need a good night's sleep."

So they locked the doors and went home.

As soon as they were out of sight, Pegleg Pete went to work. In a moment he had broken the lock and opened the doors. After another few moments, he was pushing the precious spaceship out into the night, where a big truck waited.

In the morning, when Minnie and Daisy Duck drove the boys out for their secret takeoff, the spaceship was gone! Mickey and Donald were angry.

"Look at these prints!" shouted Donald. "One shoe print and one hole—it's Pegleg Pete!"

"He'd better not take off," said Mickey. "He doesn't know our secret invention for reversing the rockets to get back. And our space suits will be too small for him when he gets to the moon."

"It would serve him right," said Donald.

"No! We've got to stop him—and save our ship!" said Mickey firmly.

So away they sped in the car, following the path of the truck up the twisting mountain road.

When they came to a stop on the hidden flying field, the spaceship was standing, poised for flight. Pegleg Pete was nowhere to be seen.

"Let's get in and start it up!" cried Donald. He and Mickey quickly climbed aboard. "Get out of here before Pegleg comes back!" Donald shouted to Daisy and Minnie as they bolted the doors behind them.

Minnie and Daisy drove to a nearby field. There they watched as the spaceship roared into the sky, spitting dust in a swirling cloud.

"Still no sign of Pegleg!" Minnie said.

"You don't suppose," cried Daisy, "that he could be aboard the ship?"

That's just where he was!

After Mickey and Donald had bolted the doors, Mickey sat down at the controls and twirled a dial to TAKEOFF. Then Donald pulled back on the rocket release. With an earsplitting roar, the spaceship lurched forward, and they saw Earth dropping away.

"What the—?" cried a loud voice. Then a face peered out of the baggage compartment. It was Pegleg Pete, waving a space gun! "What're you trying to do?" he roared. "Turn this thing around! I've just discovered there's no space suit big enough for me on board."

"We can't reverse the rockets until we get to the moon," explained Mickey Mouse.

Then, before Pegleg Pete could do any harm, Donald whacked him over the head. His heavy body sank to the floor.

"What'll we do with him now?" Donald asked.

"Just tie him up," said Mickey, "and pack him in with the supplies to keep him from freezing on the moon. We'll have to give him oxygen when we land."

When the cold, rocky landscape of the moon loomed up ahead, the two explorers were ready in their space suits.

With a thump and a bump, the spaceship clanked to a stop.

"We made it!" cried Mickey, shaking Donald's hand. "Now all we have to do is get back to Earth again."

Mickey and Donald knew that Pegleg Pete might freeze in the moon's extreme cold. There wasn't a moment to lose!

With a sure touch, they twisted the screws and tightened the bolts of the rocket reverse and hurried back to the ship.

"Wait!" cried Donald at the last minute. With a swing of his screwdriver, he cracked off a chunk of moon rock and tossed it into the ship before scrambling back in himself.

"The oxygen's getting low!" Mickey cried. "It's kept Pete going, but we'll have to get back to Earth super fast or we'll all be done for!"

With a roar, the rockets started them off. The moon glittered coldly behind them. Mickey bent over the directional finders, his face stern. One slip might mean the end for them all!

The spaceship's motion changed. Gravity was taking hold, and through the windows they saw Earth rushing up at them again. They were safe! The home field was coming into view.

What a reception awaited them when they unbolted the trusty ship's doors! What a cry went up as the heroes appeared, supporting Pegleg Pete's wobbly form.

"How did it feel to be on the moon?" a TV announcer asked.

"Fine," said Mickey, grinning broadly. "But it's better to be back home!"

Walt Disney's

LITTLE MAN OF Disneyland

Patrick Begorra woke up one bright morning feeling very fine. He fixed himself a bit of breakfast and set out for his morning stroll.

When he came to the doorway of his snug small house, at the roots of an old orange tree, Patrick stretched his arms and swelled his chest for a breath of fresh morning air. Then he lit his pipe.

But the pipe almost fell out of his mouth. And his arms froze straight out in the air, so shocked was he at the sight he saw. There were people in his orange grove—Big People striding around as if they owned the place.

Well, Patrick Begorra was not the last of the Little People left in all of Movieland for nothing! He had courage, did Patrick Begorra. So he stepped right up to those Big People to find out what this was about.

At first they wouldn't even look at him. But Patrick took care of that. He stamped down—hard—right on the foot of one.

"Ow!" cried Donald Duck. "I've been stung! Must be bees around here!" He looked down then. "What's this?" he cried. "Who in the world are you?"

"Who are you yourself, is the proper question," said Patrick Begorra right back. "This is my home, after all—has been these many years. And what, may I ask, are you doing here, acting as if you own the place, without so much as a by-your-leave from Patrick Begorra, which is me?"

“Who are we?” cried Donald Duck. “Don’t you go to the movies? Don’t you watch TV? Don’t you read books or newspapers? Don’t you know Goofy and Pluto? Don’t you know Donald Duck?”

“No,” said Patrick, and he blew a smoke ring right in Donald’s face.

"My name is Mickey Mouse, sir," said one of the other Big People, stooping down to hold out his hand. "So this is your home here, Mr. Begorra?"

"That it is," said Patrick Begorra, "and I'd like a little peace and quiet. I'll thank you all to leave at once."

"Well," said Mickey, "I'm afraid we can't do that. You see, we're going to start building here soon. Going to move all these old trees."

"Move these trees! Start building here!" cried Patrick Begorra, jumping up and down in a purple rage. "Oh, no you don't! Not while I'm around!"

"And what can you do to stop us, little fellow?" asked Donald Duck with a chuckle, leaning on his shovel in a cocky way.

"I'll show you," said Patrick, with a snap of his fingers. And down in a heap went Donald Duck. For his shovel handle had splintered—just like that.

“What happened?” cried Donald, picking himself up.

“Let that be a lesson to you,” said Patrick Begorra.

“Aw, don’t mind him,” said Goofy. “Let’s start digging up these trees.”

“And what was it you had planned to build here? Some sort of a school, perhaps?” asked Patrick.

"No, a wonderful place called Disneyland," said Mickey. "With all sorts of marvelous things for fun—a rocket trip to the moon, for one, and a wonderful Wild West stagecoach ride, a magic pirate ship that can really fly, and a trip to the mine of the Seven Dwarfs."

"Rocket trip—flying pirate ship! You must be out of your head, my boy," said Patrick Begorra. "There are no such things."

"Come along and see. We'll show you the plans. They're back at the Studio," said Mickey Mouse.

Before he knew what he was about, Patrick Begorra found himself walking along with Mickey and the rest. But he stopped short when they opened a door into a strange-looking bubble of glass.

"Oh, no you don't!" he cried in alarm. "I'll not go in there. What is it, anyway?"

"It's a helicopter, a kind of airplane. Come along for the ride," said Mickey.

When he saw all the rest of them piling in, Patrick Begorra went, too. Soon, with a whirr and a rush of blades, up went the helicopter, straight up in the air, and the ground dropped away below.

My, but you should have heard Patrick yell then! He had never dreamed of such a thing. But soon he was so busy watching the sights, as they flew over oil wells and city streets and towering brown hills, that he had no time to be scared.

Then down they swooped to the Studio. And soon Patrick found himself deep in Disneyland plans—the likes of which he had never seen.

There were rows of pretty little shops, winding rivers, an overhead railroad train—so many wonderful things to see that Patrick's head was spinning.

"And this is what you're planning to build when you root up my orange trees?" he asked.

"Yes," said Mickey. "That's our plan."

"Then go ahead, lads, if you can," said Patrick Begorra. "The place is yours. There's just one little thing I ask. May I build a wee snug little house and live there quietly after you have finished this Disneyland?"

"Fine!" said Mickey. "We'll build you the house. How about one of these?"

"No, lad, no," said Patrick Begorra. "I like a place out of sight, hidden away, so to speak."

"All right," said Mickey. "Just as you say."

So they shook hands on it. The bargain was made. They all flew back to the Disneyland site. And next morning, the work began.

Every day Patrick came out to watch. And with every day that passed, it seemed, the picture changed.

One day the railway station went up, the entrance to Disneyland.

Then, almost in the blink of an eye, Main Street was taking shape.

Soon it was time for the last tree to come out—the one with Patrick's home at its roots.

"Sorry, Pat," said Mickey, "it's got to go, but we'll find you a good new place."

"Don't bother," said Patrick. "I've picked one myself." But he would not say where his new house was.

He trundled out his household goods in his wee wheelbarrow. And all day he sat in the barrow's shade.

And at night, when everyone had gone home, Patrick wheeled his wee barrow through the shadows of Disneyland to the secret spot he'd picked for his home.

So when you visit Disneyland, keep your eyes open wide. Maybe you'll see a wee man in green, smoking a small clay pipe. Maybe you'll follow him when he goes home, and find out where he lives.

If you do, you'll be the only one in the world who's found Patrick Begorra's home!

Mad Hatter's Tea Party

10/6

There was once a Mad Hatter, a peculiar fellow who lived in a strange little house in the woods—in the woods of Wonderland.

Nearby lived a friend of his, the March Hare.

One day the March Hare heard (through the wild grapevine, of course) that it was the Mad Hatter's birthday.

So he baked and frosted a birthday cake. Then down the woodland path he went, singing as he skipped along:

"The very merriest birthday to you!
The very merriest birthday to you!"

The Mad Hatter was delighted. He called in his friend the Dormouse, a sleepy little soul, and what a jolly time they all did have!

They decided a birthday party was the best of all possible fun.

The next day, the Mad Hatter kept thinking of that party and of the jolly songs they sang. He did wish they could have another party.

The March Hare was thinking about it, too. How he longed for another piece of birthday cake!

And the sleepy Dormouse wished for another cup of tea.

But it was nobody's birthday that day.

The Mad Hatter had just had his. The March Hare's was months and months away. And the Dormouse had been so sleepy when his mother told him about his birthday that he couldn't remember it at all.

"Oh, me!" sighed the March Hare. "Nothing but un-birthdays as far as I can see. It really isn't fair. Only one birthday a year and 364 un-birthdays!"

"364 un-birthdays!" cried the Mad Hatter. "Well, fine! Splendid! Let's celebrate those!"

So they did. Every day they had an un-birthday party.

10/6

Every day they set up the table and hung up the decorations and had birthday cake and tea.

And after the party, they cleared everything away. But that soon got tiresome.

So they set up a great long table underneath the trees. They put chairs all around, and cups and plates and pots and pots of tea.

After that, they never cleared anything away. Whenever things got messy, as things at a party will, the Mad Hatter would call out, "Move down! Move down!" And the March Hare would call out, "Clean cups! Clean cups!" And away they would move, to new places at the table.

So the un-birthday party went on and on. And every day they happily sang:

"A very merry un-birthday to you!
A very merry un-birthday to you!"

All that moving got to be too much for the sleepy Dormouse. Since he was so fond of tea, he just chose himself a teapot, climbed in and stayed. Now and then he would open a drowsy eye and join in a bit of fun.

One day, a little girl named Alice wandered into Wonderland. She soon heard singing and hurried along through the trees to see what was going on.

In through the Mad Hatter's gate she stepped. Alice saw the colored lanterns hanging from the trees, and the cakes upon the table. And she heard the jolly song:

"A very merry un-birthday to you! To who?
A very merry un-birthday to me!"

Then the Mad Hatter saw her. "No room!" he cried. "What are you doing here?"

"Why, there seems to be lots of room," Alice said. "I heard singing, and it sounded so delightful—"

"It did?" cried the Mad Hatter. "What a charming child. Come in, my dear. Sit down, sit down."

"Whose birthday is it?" Alice asked as she sat in an empty chair.

"No one's. It's an un-birthday party," they said, and explained.

"Why, then it's *my* un-birthday, too," Alice said.

"A very merry un-birthday to you!" sang the Mad Hatter and the March Hare.

“Won’t you have some tea?” they asked.

“Yes, thank you,” Alice said. “Just a half cup, please.”

The Mad Hatter snatched up a carving knife and he cut a cup in two.

“My,” said Alice, “I wish Dinah were here to see this.”

“And who is Dinah?” the March Hare asked.

“Dinah is my cat,” Alice said.

"Cat! Cat! Cat!" cried a horrified voice. And the Dormouse, at the sound of that dread word, popped out of his teapot, up into the air.

Then, before Alice even sipped her tea, the March Hare pushed her and cried out, “Move down! Move down! Clean cups! Clean cups!”

“This is the silliest party I’ve ever seen,” said Alice. She walked out the gate and off through the woods. No one seemed to notice that she had left.

There they are to this very day, singing and drinking cups of un-birthday tea. If you should wander through Wonderland, perhaps you will find a little house in the woods and hear voices singing loud and free—

"A very merry un-birthday to you! To who?
A very merry un-birthday to me!"

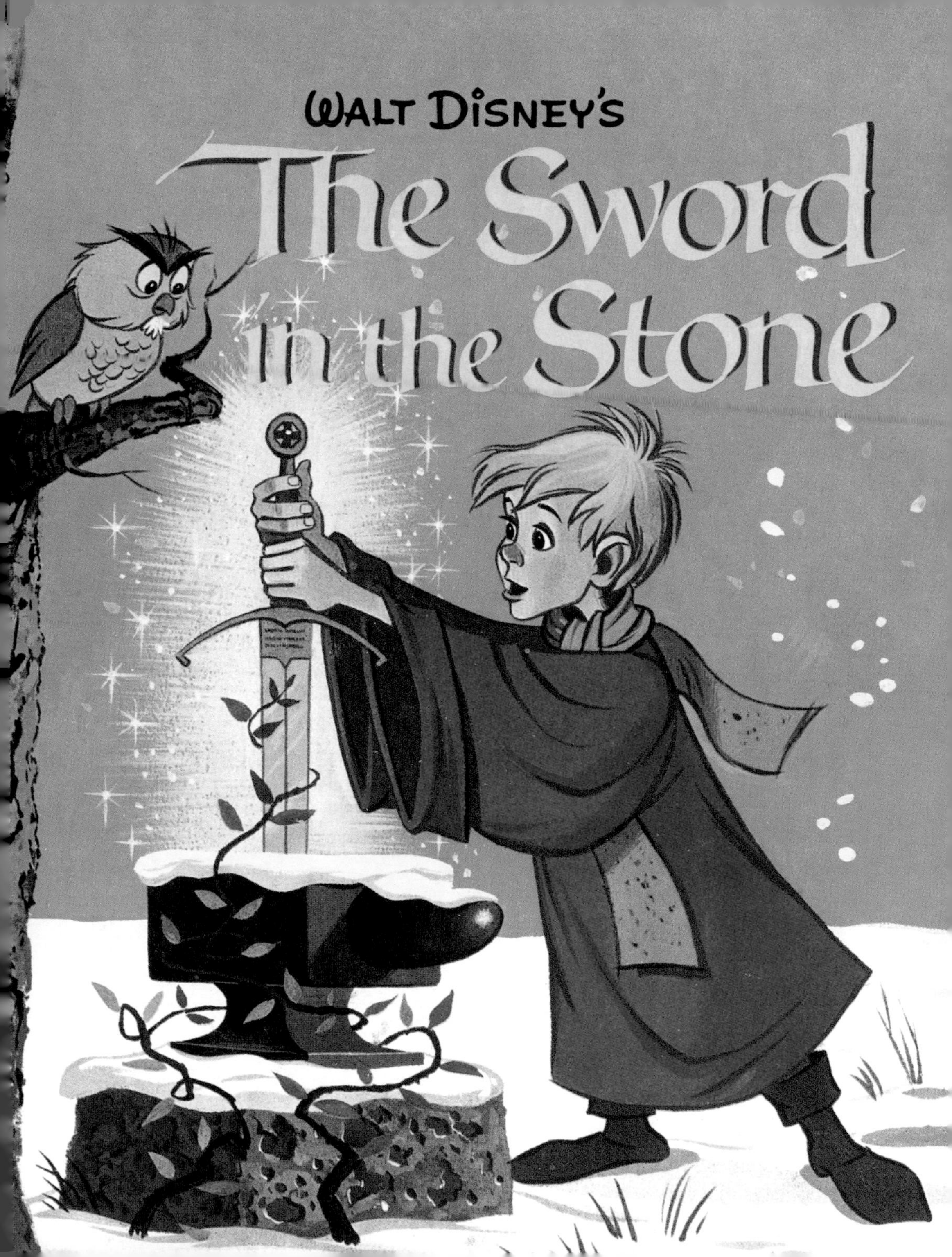
WALT DISNEY'S
The Sword in the Stone

Wart was a lonely page living in the great stone castle of Sir Ector. Nobody called Wart by his proper name, which was Arthur. Everybody called him just Wart.

Sir Ector had a big, lazy son named Kay, who liked to stretch out in the sun and doze. His favorite spot was a grassy bank near the drawbridge.

But poor Wart had to work and work.

He scrubbed pans and scoured pots in the castle cookhouse.

He helped the castle carpenter.

He polished armor
for the armorer.

He swept the castle stables clean.

Poor Wart. He was all tired out.

But one day, there was a clap of thunder in the great hall of the castle.

There was a puff of smoke—and there stood a strange old man.

"My name is Merlin. I am a wizard," he said. "Wart needs lessons. So I have come."

Sir Ector and Kay laughed and hooted.

"Lessons! What does Wart need lessons for? Go away, old man," said Sir Ector.

Merlin waved his wand. And right there inside the great hall it began to snow! It snowed and it snowed and it snowed.

Well, Sir Ector changed his mind. He let Merlin stay on and said, "Give Wart lessons, if you like."

Nobody understood why Wart needed lessons, but Merlin began to give him lessons.

He led Wart down to the moat one day. And he waved his wand.

Wart began to shrink. He shrank smaller and smaller.

Suddenly, he changed into a little fish and fell into the water.

At first it was great fun.

But then a big fish came along.

The big fish wanted to catch the little fish for lunch.

Poor little Wart. What could he do?

He used his head.

He hid in a clump of seaweed so the big fish couldn't find him.

"Very good," said Merlin. "You learned your lesson, Wart. *When in trouble, use your head.*"

Merlin kept on with the lessons. Once, he changed Wart into a squirrel.

As a squirrel, Wart stored nuts in trees. He learned to be ready for what tomorrow might bring.

Another time, Merlin changed him into a bird.

As a bird, Wart flew high in the sky. And seeing the world from way up there, he learned many things.

Wart grew wiser and wiser.

But still nobody understood. Why did Wart need lessons?

One wintry day, a knight came to the castle. He brought news of a great tournament to be held in London. The winner would be crowned king of all England!

"A tournament's the very thing we need to choose an English king," said Sir Ector. He thought that Kay would win.

And so they all rode off.

Kay sat on a prancing horse. His armor glistened in the sunlight.

But Wart was just a lowly squire. He rode a plodding donkey all the way to London town.

After many days and nights, they came at last to the tournament field. There was a blast of trumpets. And the tilting started.

Kay smiled proudly. Soon, with spear and sword, he would fight to win the crown.

Suddenly, Wart ran from the field. He had forgotten Kay's sword! It was back at the inn where they had slept.

Wart ran as fast as he could. But when he got to the inn, it was closed.

Poor Wart—where could he find a sword?

He ran and ran. In a churchyard, he saw a marble stone. On it stood a steel anvil. And stuck through the anvil was a gleaming sword.

A sword!

Wart quickly pulled it out and quickly carried it back to the tournament field.

"But that's not Kay's sword!" cried Sir Ector when he saw it.

Then he saw some letters written in gold on the sword.

This is what the letters said:

WHOSO PULLETH OUT THIS SWORD OF THIS STONE AND ANVIL IS RIGHTWISE KING BORN OF ALL ENGLAND.

Sir Ector read that. And so did all the other noblemen. Now they knew. The tournament *wasn't* the thing whereby to choose a king. *The sword was!*

But how could Wart have pulled it out? There must be some mistake.

They all went to the churchyard. Wart put back the sword into the stone.

Everyone tried, but the sword wouldn't move. Only Wart could pull it out again. So it was no mistake.

But kings must be wise. Kings must know many things. How could Wart be a king?

Wart was wise enough. And he knew enough. For that's what the lessons had been for—to prepare Wart to be king.

And Wart became a great king, known forever after as King Arthur.

Walt Disney's Cinderella's Friends

Tweet! Tweet! It is morning. At the bluebird's song, the mice in Cinderella's house wake up with squeaks and yawns.

"Today is the day!" we hear the mice say. "Today is the day of the great Mouse Ball!"

Even the bluebirds have come to help prepare. They tweet along to the chorus of the merry mouse song. This is what the mice sing:

"Cinderella, Cinderella
Is the sweetest one of all.
Now she's marrying her prince, and
So we're having a great ball!"

Some mice get busy putting up decorations. Other mice plan to get the food.

Jaq Mouse is taking a brave group down to the kitchen. And here they are, ready to start.

"Be careful!" call the decorating mice. "Be sure to watch out for the cat!"

"We will!" the brave mice promise. For they know that cat—the mean Lucifer. But away they march, right through a hole in the wall.

Down, down,
down dark tunnels,
they make their way.
And as they march,
they sing a song:

"Cinderella,
Cinderella
Is the princess
of the land,
And to make her
ball a fine one,
We will lend a
helping hand."

At last they stop. They have come to the kitchen.

"Shh!" says Jaq. And the song breaks off as he creeps out for a look around.

There, in the coziest spot of all, close to the fire, lies Lucifer Cat. But he is fast asleep.

"Come on!" Jaq signals. And the mice creep out carefully and quietly across the kitchen floor.

On the kitchen table are great riches for the Mouse Ball feast! The mice begin to climb. One, two, three, up to the chair. Four, five, six, to the tabletop. They gather as much as they can hold.

Then six, five, four, to the kitchen floor, and back, back, back toward the hole they go. But greedy Gus spies one more piece of cheese. He can't pass it up. He reaches, and—*snap!* Gus finds himself tight in a mousetrap.

Snap! Lucifer awakes! He opens one eye. The mice have vanished, all but Gus.

"Aha!" purrs Lucifer, with a horrid, hungry smile. He reaches out a paw, but he can't get the mouse out of the trap.

"Ho, hum," Lucifer thinks. "Someone will come soon and open the trap. I can have my feast then. Now I'll finish my nap."

Zzzzzz, snores Lucifer Cat. And out from their hiding places all around, hush-hush-hush, creep the mice.

They shake their heads at greedy Gus. But one, two, three,

they

spring

that

trap!

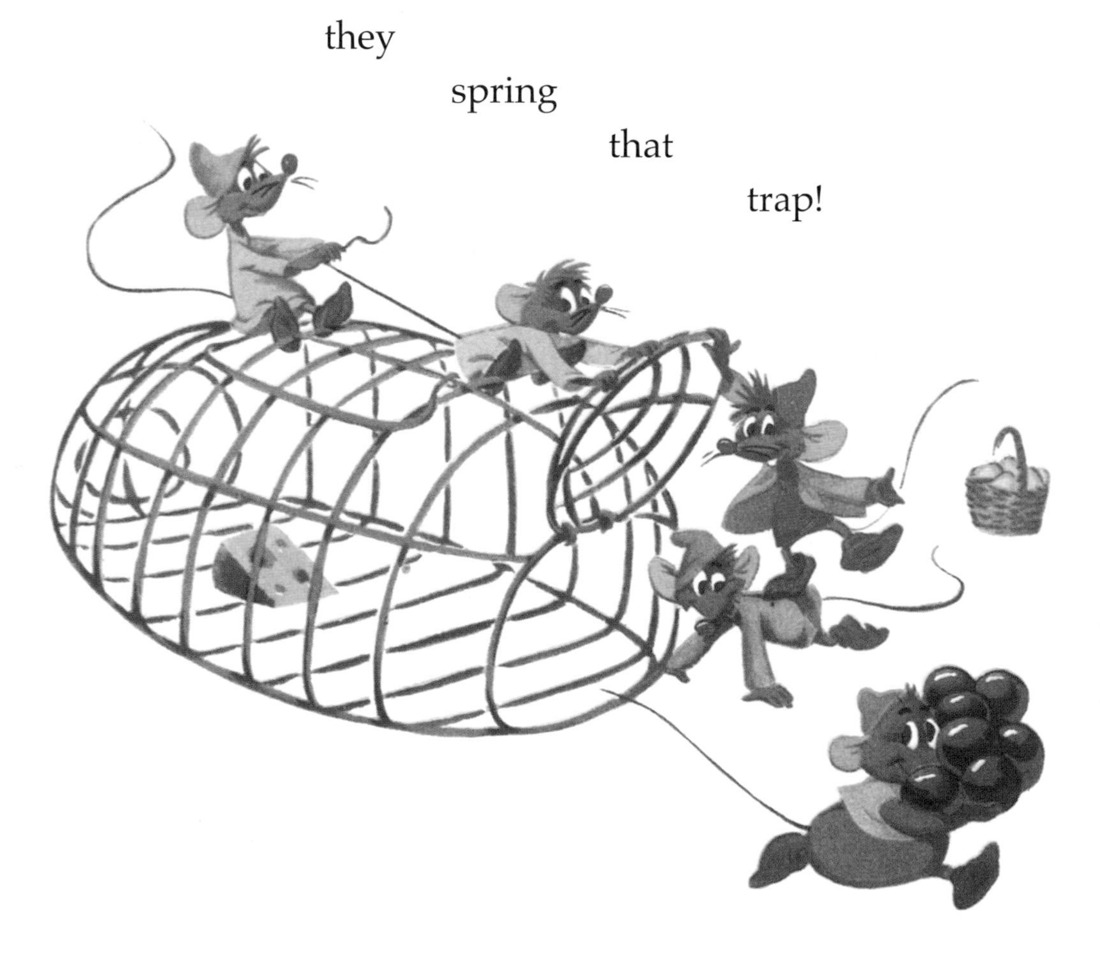

And out comes Gus with a *ping!*

Ping! Up wakes Lucifer, and there are all the mice. "Aha! I've got you now!" he thinks. And he pounces!

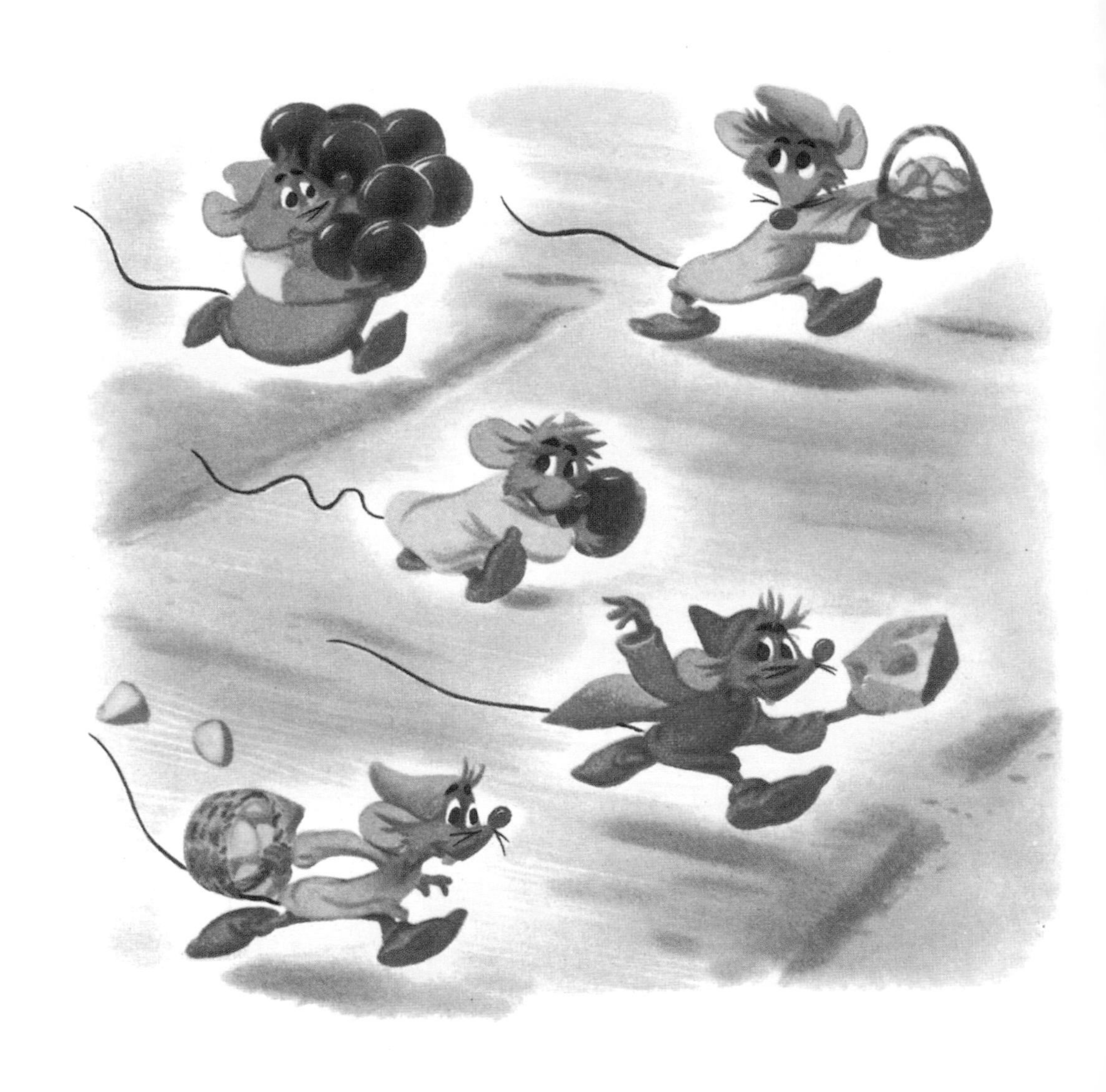

“Hurry!” cries Jaq. “Into the wall!”

The mice race for the wall, carrying what they can.

Jaq stays behind to manage Lucifer. And he leads the cat on a merry chase.

Into the hole the mice climb, one, two, three—mouse after mouse with loads of food.

Now it's Gus's turn, with his grapes piled high. But he has too many. *Plink, plunk, scatter,* down they fall!

Poor Jaq. Lucifer is getting close and Jaq is getting tired. Gus sees that his friend is in danger. What can he do?

Squish! He steps on a grape. The juice hits Lucifer in the eye. While he screeches with rage—*zip!* Up go Jaq and Gus into the hole.

Then up, up, up through the walls they go, a happy band of mice. As they climb, they sing a happy song:

"Cinderella,
Cinderella,
How we'll celebrate tonight!
We will feast and dance and frolic
By the moon and candlelight!"

And they did! There has never been a more wonderful feast, with dancing and singing and cheer.

And that's how Cinderella's mice celebrated her wedding to the prince.

WALT DISNEY'S
The Lucky Puppy

*L*ucky the puppy lived with his father, Pongo, and his mother, Perdita, and with all his sisters and brothers. The people who belonged to them were Roger and Anita and Nanny Cook. (That's Nanny Cook in the doorway above.)

Here are Penny and Lenny,
Salter and Pepper, Jolly and Rolly,
and Patch and Latch.

Here are Spot and Dot,
Blob and Blot, Blackie and Whitey,
and—where's Lucky?

Here's Lucky. He's in front of the television watching his favorite show, *Thunderbolt*.

Whenever Penny and
Lenny wanted to dig holes,

or Salter and Pepper
wanted to chew bones . . .

. . . or Patch and Latch
wanted to chase tails,

or Jolly and Rolly wanted to jump
at Nanny Cook's apron strings . . .

. . . or Spot and Dot wanted to play hide-and-seek,

or Blob and Blot wanted to growl at the mirror . . .

. . . or Blackie and Whitey wanted to take a nap,

Lucky never joined in. He just wanted to sit in front of the television watching *Thunderbolt*.

Or he practiced tricks he saw on television. "I'm going to be a television star," said Lucky.

Well, all the other puppies learned puppy tricks. Soon they could sit up and roll over.

They could dance
and shake hands.

They could jump for a treat
and walk politely on a leash.

But not Lucky. He was too busy dreaming about being a television star.

One day, he decided he was ready to be in a television show. So he slipped out of the house and ran down the street.

He ran around a corner. And there he stopped. He was lost. He didn't know his way to the television place. And he didn't know his way home.

Poor Lucky. He walked and walked and walked. He tried to show people his television tricks. But they didn't understand.

"He doesn't seem to know any regular puppy tricks," the people said.

Finally, a policeman came along. He looked at Lucky's tag. And he took Lucky home.

There were Penny and Lenny, Salter and Pepper, Jolly and Rolly, Patch and Latch . . .

Spot and Dot, Blob and Blot, and Blackie and Whitey, all doing puppy tricks for treats. But not Lucky.

Lucky was all tired out.
He crept straight into his basket.
And he went to sleep.

He even slept through the *Thunderbolt* show while the other puppies watched.

But the next morning, Lucky was up bright and early. “Time enough for television later,” he said. “Now I am going to learn my puppy tricks.” And he did!

WALT DISNEY'S

Mary Poppins

It was morning on Cherry Tree Lane. Admiral Boom had shot off his morning cannon to give the day a proper start. Miss Lark, in the biggest house on the Lane, had sent her dog, Andrew, out for his morning stroll.

But in the nursery at Number Seventeen Cherry Tree Lane, Jane and Michael Banks were still in bed.

"Up, up!" said Mary Poppins, their nanny, pulling back the blankets with a firm hand. "We'll have no lounging about on a super-cali-fragi-listic-expi-ali-do-cious day."

"Super-cali-what, Mary Poppins?" asked Michael.

"Close your mouth, Michael. We are not a codfish. Super-cali-fragi-listic-expi-ali-do-cious, of course. If you can't think of a word that says just what you want to say, try super-cali-fragi-listic-expi-ali-do-cious. And it *just* describes today."

That got Jane and Michael up and dressed and breakfasted in record time.

"Out to the park we go," said Mary Poppins, hurrying them into their hats and coats. "Spit-spot, this way."

"Super-cali-fragi-listic-expi-ali-do-cious!" sang Jane and Michael as they marched along the Lane. They almost bumped into Mary Poppins when she stopped to speak to Andrew, Miss Lark's little dog.

"Yip yap yap," said Andrew.

"Slower, please," said Mary Poppins. "I can't understand a word you say."

"Yip yap yap," said Andrew, slower.

"Again?" said Mary Poppins.

"Yap yap," said Andrew.

“Yes, of course,” said Mary Poppins. “I’ll go straightaway. And thank you very much.”

“Yap,” said Andrew.

Then, taking Jane and Michael by the hand, Mary Poppins started off the way Andrew had come.

“What did he say?” asked Jane.

“He said, ‘You’re welcome,’” said Mary Poppins.

“But what else did he say?” Jane insisted.

"I don't think he said anything at all," said Michael crossly. "And I thought we were going for a walk in the park."

"There's been a change of plans," said Mary Poppins. "Come along, please. Don't straggle."

She led them at a brisk pace down narrow, twisting streets they had never seen before. Then she stopped at the door of a small house.

Rap, rap went the parrot's-head handle of Mary Poppins' umbrella. The door was opened by Mary's friend Bert.

"How is he?" Mary Poppins asked.

Bert shook his head. "Never seen him like this," he said. "And that's the truth."

Mary Poppins led Jane and Michael inside the house. They found themselves in a large, cheerful room. In the center stood a table set for tea.

"Bless my soul," gurgled a voice rich with chuckles. "Is that Mary Poppins? I'm delighted to see you, my dear."

Jane and Michael looked about. They could see no one else in the room.

"Uncle Albert, you promised not to go floating around again!" she said. And she seemed to be speaking to the ceiling.

Jane and Michael looked up. There in the air sat Mary Poppins' uncle Albert, chuckling merrily.

"I know, my dear," said Uncle Albert, wiping a merry eye. "I tried—really, I did. But I do so enjoy laughing, you know." Here the chuckles bubbled up so that he bobbed against the ceiling. "And the moment I start—*hee, hee*—it's all *up* with me." To the children he whispered, "It's laughing that does it, you know."

Jane and Michael were trying hard to be polite. They kept their faces straight. But first the laughter sparkled out of their eyes. Then it bubbled up their throats. They began to chuckle.

By this time Bert was rolling about, shaking with laughter. As they watched, he rose into the air and soon was bobbing about beside Uncle Albert.

Michael's chuckle grew to a laugh. So did Jane's. Soon they were simply filled with laughter. It bubbled out, and they felt lighter and lighter until their feet left the floor and they floated up to the ceiling!

"How nice," said Uncle Albert. "I was hoping you'd turn up. Do make yourselves comfortable, my dears."

"I must say you're a sight, the lot of you," said Mary Poppins, her arms folded in a way that Jane and Michael knew meant she disapproved.

"You know, speaking of sights," said Bert, "that reminds me of my brother who has a nice cushy job in a watch factory."

"Is that so?" said Uncle Albert. "What does he do?"

"You know what he does?" gasped Bert, who was laughing so hard he could scarcely speak. "He stands around in this watch factory all day and *makes faces.*"

At that, all four of them roared so with laughter that they turned somersaults in the air.

"I found a horseshoe today," said Bert, holding his sides. "You know what that means?"

"I certainly do," said Uncle Albert. "It means that some poor horse is walking around in his stocking feet."

Again the room rocked with laughter. Only Mary Poppins looked stern.

"Most disgraceful thing I've ever seen," she snapped, "or my name isn't Mary Poppins."

"Speaking of names," said Bert, "I know a man with a wooden leg named Smith. . . ."

"Really?" chortled Uncle Albert. "What's the name of his other leg?"

More gusts of laughter.

"Now then, Jane, Michael! It is time for tea," said Mary Poppins firmly from below. "I will not have my schedule disrupted."

"Oh, please stay!" begged Uncle Albert. He pointed at the table on the floor. "I have a splendid tea waiting for us—if you could, er, manage to get the table to . . ."

With a rattle and a bump, the table began to jerk. Then up it rose through the air—cups, cakes, teapot, and all.

"Oh, splendid, splendid! Thank you, my dear," said Uncle Albert. Then, to Michael and Jane, "Keep your feet back, my dears. Watch the cups and mind the jam."

"Next thing, I suppose you'll be wanting me to pour," said Mary Poppins with a sigh. And up she floated, neat as you please, without so much as a smile.

The others still laughed and bobbled about as Mary Poppins poured and passed the tea—with milk for Michael and Jane.

"Thank you, my dear," said Uncle Albert. "I'm having such a good time. I wish you could all stay up here with me always."

"We'll jolly well have to." Michael grinned. "There's no way to get down."

"Well, to be honest," said Uncle Albert, "there *is* a way. Just think of something sad and down you go."

But who could think of anything sad? They chuckled at the very idea.

"Time to go home!" Mary Poppins' voice, crisp and firm, cut sharply through the laughter.

And suddenly, at that sad thought, down came Jane and Michael, Uncle Albert and Bert, *bump, bump, bump, bump* on the floor.

“Good-bye,” said Michael. “We’ll be back soon.”

“And thank you,” said Jane soberly. “We’ve had a lovely time.”

“Oh, dear.” Uncle Albert was sobbing as he waved good-bye. “It makes me so sad to see them leave.”

Back home, Jane and Michael tried to tell their father about their adventure.

"We floated in the air and had tea on the ceiling," Jane began.

"And there was this man with a wooden leg named Smith," Michael broke in.

"Poppins!" cried Mr. Banks. "What is the meaning of this?"

"Children will be children," sniffed Mary Poppins. "And these two are up past their bedtime. Spit-spot." And she marched them off to the nursery, muttering, "The very idea!"

Michael and Jane just looked at each other.

"Anyway," said Jane, kicking off a slipper, "it was a super-cali-fragi-listic-expi-ali-do-cious day!"

Walt Disney's

Sleeping Beauty

AND THE GOOD FAIRIES

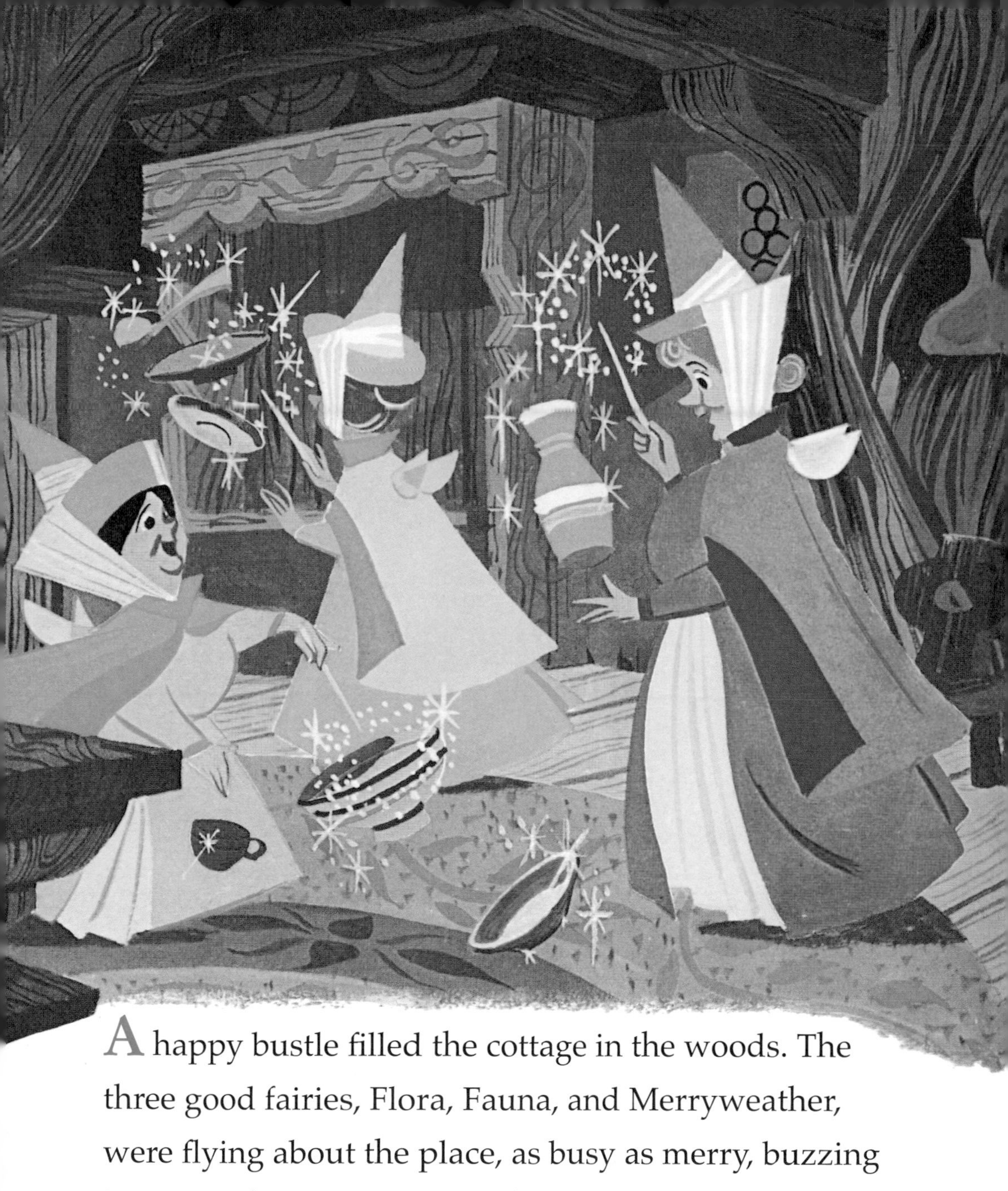

A happy bustle filled the cottage in the woods. The three good fairies, Flora, Fauna, and Merryweather, were flying about the place, as busy as merry, buzzing bees. For the first time since her marriage to Prince Phillip, Princess Aurora was coming to visit them!

So Flora waved her wand over the woodland flowers until each blossom glowed like a bit of rainbow.

Fauna worked her magic on the baby birds, teaching them to twitter a welcome song.

And Merryweather, with the help of the breezes, swept and dusted the little cottage until it shone with a magic glow.

It was in this very cottage that the three fairies had raised the little Princess from her christening day. And now she was coming to visit them here. And they were to go on with her to the castle of the King and Queen, to deck it out with magic for the homecoming feast.

It was Merryweather who first heard the *clippety-clop* of distant hooves and the rumble of wheels on the royal coach, far down the forest road.

"Come, come, girls!" Merryweather cried. "She's almost here. There's no time to lose!"

Quickly she bent over the well beside the cottage for a glance at her reflection in the water below. *Plink!* Into the well fell her magic wand. But Merryweather was too excited to notice that.

Up bustled Fauna, puffing just a bit. "Oh me!" she cried. "Do I look all right?"

Over the well she bent for a glimpse. But just then, the coachman's horn sounded loud and clear, off among the trees. So Fauna did not hear the *plink* as her magic wand dropped into the well.

Next came Flora, trying to be calm.

"The dear girl," she fluttered. "How sweet of her to want to see us and the cottage again. But remember, we must not keep her long. For the King and Queen will be waiting at the castle."

As she spoke, she caught sight of the royal carriage approaching at last.

"Oh," she cried. "Is my cap on straight?"

She bent to look, then turned toward the road as the coach came to a halt. And into the well, all unseen, fell a third magic wand!

"Flora! Fauna! Merryweather!" cried a voice they loved. And down from the coach stepped Princess Aurora, into the good fairies' arms.

Together they went into the little cottage where they had lived for so many happy years.

"How lovely it is," said the happy Princess. "Just as I remembered it—and so are you sweet three!"

“Well, my dear,” said Flora briskly. “Now we must all be on our way. For your father and mother have kindly invited us to come to the castle with you, and to decorate it for the homecoming feast.”

"Lovely," said the Princess. "You'll decorate it with your magic wands. Where are they, by the way?"

"Right here," said Merryweather. "Why, we wouldn't be without them, you know."

"No indeed," said Fauna. "Always right at hand—"

"But they aren't!" said Flora. "Where are those wands?"

Well, they looked high and low, inside the cottage and out. But not a sign of them could they find.

"We cannot disappoint the King and Queen," cried Merryweather.

"And everyone in the countryside," added Fauna.

"We must find them!" said Flora firmly. "Now let's think. What were we doing last with them?"

"You were brightening up the woodland flowers," said Merryweather.

So they hunted through the woods. But Flora's wand was not there.

"You were teaching the baby birds a welcome song," they reminded Fauna.

So they hunted among the bushes and trees. They searched every bird's nest around. But Fauna's wand was not there.

"You, Merryweather, were sweeping out the cottage with the help of the little breezes."

So they hunted all through the cottage again. But the wand was nowhere to be seen.

Now the sun was sinking beyond the deep woods. At the castle, everyone would be waiting, they knew. What in the world could they do?

"I know," said Princess Aurora. "I'll ask the Wishing Well."

So over the Wishing Well's edge she bent.

"Why, it's all a-sparkle with sunbeams," she cried. "And starlight and rainbows—deep inside the well!"

"Our wands!" cried the fairies.

Tugging all together on the rope, they pulled up the bucket in the well. Up it came, full to the brim with magic wands and sunbeams and such.

Then into the carriage the four of them flew. And away went the horses, *clippety-clip*, off to the castle. It soon was aglow with sunbeams and starlight—and lovelight, too, for Princess Aurora's homecoming. And a lovely time was had by all.

WALT DISNEY'S THE Ugly Duckling

One lovely summer afternoon, a mother duck sat on her nest. In the nest, warm and snug, were five beautiful eggs. The mother duck sat very still, waiting for the eggs to hatch into five little ducklings.

At last the mother gave a quack of joy and sprang off the nest. The eggs were rocking back and forth. From inside them came pecking and scratching sounds. The mother duck bent over to watch.

Then one, two, three, four eggs cracked open. And out tumbled four tiny ducklings, yellow as butter and soft as down, with bright eyes and cute little bills.

They all stood up and looked around. Then with soft little quacks they climbed out of the nest and waddled around in the shade.

What a beautiful family! the mother duck thought.

But then she looked at the nest and sadly shook her head. For the fifth and biggest egg had not hatched yet.

So she sat down again and waited some more. Soon the big egg showed signs of life.

In a moment, two feet broke through the shell. Then a head appeared. But instead of being small and yellow and downy like the other ducklings, it was big and white and fuzzy.

"Honk!" said the new duckling, eager to be liked.

"Horrors!" said the mother duck. "He doesn't sound like any child of mine."

"Quack!" said the other ducklings. "He's funny-looking, too. We don't want to play with an Ugly Duckling."

And they waddled away with their mother.

The Ugly Duckling couldn't understand why everyone had left him alone. He followed the others down to the pond.

There he found the mother duck. She was swimming around the pond with the four little ducklings on her back.

The Ugly Duckling honked at them, hoping for a ride. But the mother duck just scowled at him and told him to go away.

Poor Ugly Duckling! There he sat, all alone at the edge of the pond.

Why won't they play with me? he wondered sadly. *Why do they call me ugly?* Big tears filled his eyes and trickled down to splash in the pond.

The Ugly Duckling, glancing down, saw a strange sight. There was his own reflection, all blurred and twisted with the ripples of the water.

"Oh, dear!" cried the Ugly Duckling. "I am ugly indeed. I will run away and hide where no one will see me."

So he turned away from the sunny pond and went slowly into the dark and gloomy forest.

How sad he felt there, alone in the forest, with the silent shadows looming all around.

But after a while, he heard a friendly chirping. Baby birds were calling from their cozy nest.

They sound nice, thought the Ugly Duckling. *Maybe they will play with me.*

So he hopped and scrambled into the nest with them.

The baby birds liked him. "And our mother will like you, too," they promised.

The Ugly Duckling could hardly wait for the mother bird to come. Soon she came flying in with a big juicy worm in her beak. *Snap!* went the Ugly Duckling's hungry beak as he snatched up that whole big worm.

The mother bird was furious. She pulled the worm away from him.

"Get out of here, you ugly thing!" she cried as she chased the frightened Ugly Duckling out of the nest.

The Ugly Duckling rushed to the pond as fast as he could go.

Everyone hates me because I'm ugly, he thought. Then he lay down on a log and cried.

"Honk! Honk! Honk! Honk!" The Ugly Duckling heard the sound over his crying. He blinked away his tears and shyly looked around.

There, right in front of him, paddling in the water, were four fuzzy white creatures just like him!

"What's the matter, crying on a beautiful day like this?" they asked. "Come on in and play with us."

The Ugly Duckling dove off the log and they all began to play. But in the midst of a lively game of water tag, his playmates suddenly swam away, honking happily.

The Ugly Duckling looked up and saw—
the most beautiful bird in the world.

"Mother! Mother!" his new friends cried. "We've found a new little brother to play with."

"Welcome home," said the beautiful snow-white swan, cradling the Ugly Duckling in her wing. "You are a fine, handsome baby swan, and you'll someday be King of the Pond."

From the shore, the mother duck and her downy yellow babies watched the Ugly Duckling's welcome.

"Come back and play with us!" they called.
But the little Ugly Duckling sailed happily away with the swans.